I LOVED YOU, YOU NEVER LOVED ME

I LOVED YOU, YOU NEVER LOVED ME

Viktor Zubin

I Loved You, You Never Loved Me

Copyright © 2023 by Viktor G. Zubin. All rights reserved.

No part of this publication may be reproduced, stored in a retrieval system or transmitted in any way by any means, electronic, mechanical, photocopy, recording or otherwise without the prior permission of the author except as provided by USA copyright law.

The opinions expressed by the author are not necessarily those of URLink Print and Media.

1603 Capitol Ave., Suite 310 Cheyenne, Wyoming USA 82001
1-888-980-6523 | admin@urlinkpublishing.com

URLink Print and Media is committed to excellence in the publishing industry.

Book design copyright © 2023 by URLink Print and Media. All rights reserved.

Published in the United States of America

ISBN 978-1-68486-610-6 (Paperback)
ISBN 978-1-68486-491-1 (Digital)

12.07.23

AUTHOR'S NOTE

The story in this book, as well as the characters are based on a true story. Some events were added for dramatic effect, while others were altered. Since the characters are based on real people their names are changed for confidentiality purposes.

PROLOGUE

March 1st, 2010

"LADIES AND GENTLEMEN! WELCOME TO THE ANNUAL COLLEGE BASKETBALL CHAMPIONSHIP! Today is the day you have all been waiting for, THE WILDCATS VS THE TIMBERWOLVES! These two teams have a rivalry unlike any other, and today we finally get to see them in action. The team that wins the championship has a chance to play on the national team. From there, the teams may get a chance to go pro basketball. ARE YOU READY TO SEE WHO WILL BECOME A CHAMPION?" The whole crowd roared in response and everyone waited in anticipation as the first team entered the stadium.

Chapter

1

CHILDHOOD FRIENDS

March 1, 2000

"Max! It's dinner time!"

"Oh come on mom, 30 more minutes please" Max stood in his backyard, holding a basketball, begging his mother to let him play a little bit longer. His mom, Anna, looked at him with love in her eyes and said, "30 minutes. No more, no less. It's getting dark soon." Anna continued to set up the table for dinner.

Anna's husband, John, was not in the picture. He died a year ago from blood cancer.

"Thanks mom" Max turned around and continued to practice shooting in the basket. Max always made sure to challenge himself by increasing the distance from the basket. Max loved basketball more than anything in the world.

His father, John, always wanted to be a professional athlete in basketball. He even trained very hard for it. However, when he went to the tryouts, he was told that even though he was in good shape, he was too old to compete professionally.

From that moment on, Max decided to become a professional basketball player. Unfortunately, John succumbed to cancer when Max was seven years old. If before Max was giving 100% of his energy to training, then after his father passed away he gave 200%. Nothing could distract him from his goal.

After 30 minutes Max came into the house and prepared to have dinner saying, "Jake is going to come over to play basketball with me tomorrow, is that alright?"

"Of course it is sweetheart. I know how much you love basketball. Make sure not to overdue it ok."

"Ok mom"

"Also, make sure to take a shower before you go to sleep"

"Got it"

After dinner, Max watched his favorite movie of all time, *The Lion King(1994)*. After Max finished the movie, he took a shower and went to sleep.

The next day, Jack came over and they had basketball practice in the backyard. "Let's alternate between offense and defense. You go first, I will defend." said Max.

"Alright, you better prepare yourself, because I won't hold back.". The boys continued in this manner day in and day out, playing basketball from dawn 'till dusk. Anna stood there watching in the window and felt proud because she saw that her son was determined and gave it his all.

(10 years later. Basketball match)

"60 SECONDS REMAINING! The WildCats have got the ball, but will they score in time? The score is 14:16. They need a three pointer to win the game. If they win, then they get a chance to play for the World Championship! However, the question remains; will they make a comeback? One thing is certain; Max, the Captain of the WildCats, and Jack, the vice-captain are the aces of the team."

"AND HE SCORES! LADIES AND GENTLEMEN! HE DID IT AGAIN! HOW DOES HE DO IT? If I hadn't known any better, I would say that Max has a God-given talent for basketball. Well that settles it. THE WILDCATS ADVANCE TO PLAY THE WORLD CHAMPIONSHIP MATCH!"

The crowd roared in approval as many started chanting, "WILDCATS! WILDCATS! WILDCATS!". Meanwhile, Max and his team exited the high school stadium.

Chapter

2

TRAGEDY STRIKES

(The Timberwolves' locker room, Before the big game)

"Who are you? What are you doing here?" said one of the TimberWolves.

"I am here to make a deal with your capitan."

The TimberWolves looked at the man suspiciously, "Ross, some dude here wants to talk to you!" After that, a tall blonde man walked to the center of the locker room, and looked at the man from top to bottom.

"Aren't you Jake from the WildCats? What does the mighty vice-captain want with us?" Asked Ross, mockery evident in his tone.

Jake took a deep breath and said, "I can guarantee you a victory during the World Championship"

"Really? How would you do that? Are you saying that you are willing to betray your team?"

"Exactly. I am tired of being second to Max. We used to be friends at one point, but not anymore. The way I see it, Max needs to be crippled" There was hatred in Jake's eyes. Hearing what Jack had to say, Ross laughed uncontrollably saying, "looks like the WildCats are not as,perfect as they seem." Then Ross turned to Jake and said to him, "Do what you suggested, we will focus on the game." With that, the TimberWolves headed off to practice. Soon only Jake was left in the locker rooms with an evil smile on his face. *This time I will be in the spotlight Max.* Thinking about the glory he was going to receive, Jake walked out of the TimberWolves' locker room.

The WildCats entered the college stadium. As they entered, cheers were heard and some people chanted, "WILDCATS! WILDCATS! WILDCATS!". Meanwhile on the other side of the stadium, the same thing happened for the TimberWolves. The announcer proudly introduced both teams receiving even more cheers from the crowd. Max waited in anticipation for the start of the match. *Finally I will achieve my dream. All that stands between me and my dream is this game. With* renewed determination, Max went out to start the first half.

Everything went as planned. The WildCats got an early lead on the TimberWolves. The crowd cheered non-stop. Everyone was convinced that the WildCats had the game in the bag.

During the second half, everything changed. The most confused was Max. Every time he passed a ball to one of his teammates, he would find a way to fumble the ball away. From a 12-man team, the WildCats turned into a one-man team. Max was good at the game, but alone there is very little that can do. Soon enough the TimberWolves caught up to the WildCats on the Scoreboard. The score was 19:19. Due to the score being dead even, the game went into Overtime. Three minutes were added to the game clock. During overtime, the TimberWolves were crushing their opposition. However, despite being essentially down 11 people, Max managed to stay one point behind the TimberWolves. He was nicknamed, "The Sniper" for a reason.

Seeing the dire situation and wanting to keep his word to the Timberwolves, Jake decided to stop hiding his hostility towards Max. There were 60 seconds left on the game clock. Max needed one more point to tie the match to go to the free throw. Max was preparing to throw the ball. However, before he could do so, he was tackled. Max heard something snap. He wasn't sure what it was. One thing is for sure though, Max couldn't get up. He groaned and moaned in pain. The crowd was shocked beyond belief. They could not believe what they were seeing. The stadium split in two. Some were cheering for the victory of the TimberWolves, while others were booing for the defeat of the WildCats. Soon an ambulance arrived and carried Max on a stretcher. Then they hurried to the ER. By this time Max was unconscious because of the pain. The only one who was smiling throughout the whole accident was Jack, the vice-captain of the WildCats.

Chapter

3

IT CAN'T GET ANY WORSE, CAN IT?

Max woke up confused. Everything was different. Max looked around wondering, *Where am I?* Before he could fully comprehend what was happening, a nurse came in panic on her face saying, "Sir, you need to lay down" "Where am I?"

As the nurse checked on Max's condition she answered, "You are in an emergency room. Wait here I will call the doctor"

Soon the doctor walked into the room. "Hey Max I see that you're up. We need to talk. I have good news and bad news. The good news is that the surgery has gone well. You are quite lucky that your leg has broken cleanly and that I wasn't smashed into smithereens. The bad news is that I would not recommend participating in any physical sport from this day forward. Reason being, you were lucky this time, but if something like this happens again, then there's a high chance that you will be crippled forever" When Max heard the doctor's verdict, he was shocked beyond belief. No words could describe his pain. *No more basketball. All my hopes and dreams are gone.* Before he noticed, hot tears streamed down his face. *Can this day get any worse?* At that moment, there was a knock on the door. "Hello, may I come in?" The angelic voice belonged to Lilly, Max's girlfriend. Lily was a blonde with an alluring figure and a nice smile. The doctor went to greet Lily.

"How may I help you?" He asked.

"I am here to see Max. I am his girlfriend."

"Max is recovering from a surgery. He needs to rest"

"A surgery! How come I wasn't informed of this? Can I see him please?" There was panic in her voice. Seeing this, the doctor took pity on Lily and said, "make it quick" With that Lily sprinted into the room and fell on Max's bedside, "Thank goodness you're alright!" She said, tearing up. Seeing the scene in front of him Max was touched. "Don't worry, with a little bit of rehab I will be up and running in no time" he said reassuring her. "However…" Max paused, unsure how to continue, "…the doctor said that I will have to give up on any physical sport, otherwise I risk becoming a cripple." When Lily heard everything that Max said her face changed. "So you are useless" Lily mumbled to herself which was barely audible. Max was confused at first. However, confusion was quickly replaced by shock. "What do you mean 'useless'?" He asked, hoping that he misheard. But what he heard next shocked him to the core. "I said you are USELESS! Did you not hear me the first time? Max, you are a great guy, but you and I, we're over. Don't call me anymore." With those words Lily stormed out of the room in a hurry. Everything happened too quickly. One moment Lily is crying on Max's bedside, and the next she looks at him with scorn and leaves the room. The doctor came back into the room. There is no sign of the girlfriend anywhere. Max is sitting on the bed staring at a wall with tears running down his cheeks.

Chapter

4

THE PURPOSE OF LIFE

You are useless. You can no longer play basketball, otherwise you will risk becoming a cripple. Everything is dark. Max is running towards the ball, but everytime he gets close to it, the ball disappears.

Max jumps out of bed with sweat all over his body. After 6 months of intense rehab, Max has gotten to a decent physical shape. The only thing left to remind Max of the tragedy was a scar on his dominant right leg. However, even though his physical condition was decent, his mental condition deteriorated sufficiently. Max refused to be admitted to a mental hospital stating that he is not crazy and that they don't know what he has been through, so they don't understand. Ever since the tragedy a half a year ago, Max kept having the same nightmare every night. This nightmare would spoil the rest of the day for Max, to the point where he couldn't fully concentrate on anything. In addition, Max would get easily angered for the smallest of things especially if those things didn't go his way. *I can't live like this anymore. Without basketball, I have no purpose in life.* With those dark thoughts in his head Max went to the bathroom planning to suffocate himself in the bathtub by holding his breath. He filled the bathtub with water and got into the bathtub. He got as much air in his lungs as he possibly could without the intention to come back for air. Max was pretty good at holding his breath underwater. However, his best was a measly 60 seconds underwater. He submerged himself in water and started counting out of habit. When Max got to 60 seconds, he could barely hold his breath. *Goodbye World!* Just when Max thought that he would enter the afterlife, his head was forcibly lifted out of the water. Max started to deeply inhale the oxygen. When he was able to focus again he was shocked. His mom stared at him with the same shock and tears in her eyes. "WHAT WERE YOU TRYING TO DO! KILL YOURSELF! YOU ARE SELFISH!" Anna yelled at her son through the tears.

"You don't get it mom. Without Basketball I AM NOTHING! I HAVE NO PURPOSE IN LIFE ANYMORE! I AM USELESS!"

At this point Anna was even more angry with her son, "SO WHAT IF YOU CAN'T PLAY BASKETBALL ANYMORE! IT DOESN'T MEAN YOU GO KILLING YOURSELF! FIND A NEW PURPOSE IN LIFE!" When Max heard that, he was stunned for a second. *Mom is right! If Basketball is out of the equation, then I need to replace it with something else.* With renewed determination Max looked at his mom with guilt in his eyes, "Mom I am so sorry. I have made you go through hell because of me. Please forgive me. I was so focused on basketball, trying to fulfill dads' dream, that I disregarded any other options. " By the time Max finished speaking, tears were streaming down his face. Seeing this, Anna pulled her son into a hug and patted his head saying, "Of course I forgive you. You are my son after all, how could I not forgive you?" For what seemed like an eternity, both mother and son stood there in the bathroom, in each other's embrace until the doorbell rang. Both Anna and Max snapped back to their senses. "I'll go get that" said Anna rushing to the door. When she opened the door, there stood a middle-aged man with streaks of silver in his hair. He was wearing a suit and a tie, and looked professional.

"Does Max live here? If you wouldn't mind, may I please talk to him"

Chapter

5

NEW OPPORTUNITY & HOPE

Three people sat in a semicircle at the kitchen table. Both Anna and Max waited patiently for the man to speak. "Allow me to Introduce myself. My name is Frank. I am the current CEO of an oil company. We are currently expanding and I would like to hire Max as an intern."

"I am confused. Why would you hire me?" Asked Max.

"To tell you the truth, your father and I were best friends. I am a fan of basketball. Unfortunately, I paled in comparison to your father when it comes to basketball. It was then that I decided to start my own business. As it turns out, I struck gold after countless failures and misfortunes. My men found an oil spring. Using that oil, I became a wealthy man. We have expanded into areas before. Therefore, when the oil rig dries up, the company will be fine. The reason why I came personally to offer you a job is because I know what happened to you. I watched it happen live. I knew at that point that most likely, the door to professional basketball will close forever. So, what do you say? Will you come work with me?" Everyone stayed silent for a while. Max sighed deeply and said, "You have no idea what this means for me! Of course I will!" Then he paused in thought and said, "What about my mom? Where will she stay while I am working for you?" "You guys can stay with my wife and I at our mansion. We have a daughter your age. If you're lucky you will get to meet her. Come, I have a private jet prepared." With that Frank stood up from the table and headed towards the front door. Meanwhile, both Max and Anna were shocked by what they heard. *Mansion? Private jet? Is that even possible?* Both stood up to follow Frank but they couldn't move. They were frozen in a stupor.

"Are you coming or not?" Frank asked, standing next to the front door. Frank's voice snapped both Max and Anna out of their frozen state and they quickly followed behind him. Then Frank added, "Don't forget to grab all the important documents and don't worry, everything else will be provided at the mansion."

"Where are we going?" asked Max out of curiosity.

"St. Louis, Missouri"

EPILOGUE

(10 years later)

"Did you get everything you needed?"

"Yes I did, thanks to you. Oh Rose, what I do without you" Both Max and Rose stopped packing and looked at each other lovingly. Max was the first to break eye-contact and said with sadness in his voice, "Rose please don't look at me like that,if you do then, I won't be able to leave for the business trip. You know that ever since dad(Frank) retired as the CEO of the company, I am now fully responsible for the company as the new CEO". Rose finished packing the luggage and said while walking over to Max, "I am well aware of your new responsibilities Mr. CEO. However you do realize that az your wife and lover I am worried about your well-being. The last thing I want is to lose my dear husband." With that Rose tidied up Max's blue suit as well as the tie. Max was deeply touched by Rose' words. He gently touched Rose's cheek saying, "I know you are, and I'm grateful for it. You and the kids are the only reason I have to return home." Max looked passionately into the eyes of his wife.

"Speaking of kids" Rose leaned closer and whispered into Max's ear, "I am pregnant". Max's eyes almost popped out of their sockets, "Again?"

Rose nodded her head shyly. "How far along?"

Rose lifted two fingers saying, "two weeks". Instantly the shock on Max's face was replaced by a wide grin. "WE'RE GONNA HAVE A BABY!" With those words Max proceeded to passionately kiss his wife.

"Daddy, it's not fair I want to kiss mommy too!" All of a sudden a two-year-old child rushed in and jumped in between Max and Rose. Max turned towards the two-year-old child, squared down and said, "John, why don't you call your brother and sisters."

"Ok" John said innocently and ran off to do as he was told. Max turned back towards Rose and said, "I will make sure to return in a week tops. I love you."

"I love you too". Max and Rose were about to kiss again when Alex, Gloria, and Michelle entered the bedroom. "You called for us dad?"Asked Alex, taking the role of a representative.

"Yes I did. I have good news and I have bad news. The good news is that soon you guys will have a little brother or sister." When the kids heard that they clapped and cheered saying, "Yay"

"The bad news is that I have to leave on a business trip for a week. That's why I need your help to protect mom while

I'm away. Can I count on you guys"

"Sir, yes sir!" The children exclaimed.

"Gloria, Michelle I have an additional assignment for you.

Help mom around the house ok?"

"Ok daddy, leave it to us!" The girls exclaimed for the second time.

"Finally, remember, WORK AS A TEAM!" The whole family exclaimed in unison.

"Thank you Mr. Max. We are glad that our company is getting an owner like you. Unfortunately for us, we lost our business to the competition. Otherwise we wouldn't be forced to sell the business. We hope that Mr. Max will have better luck in running a business in Minnesota."

"Don't worry sires, my.team and I have it under control". With that, Max shook hands with Mark, the CEO and Michael, the

Vice-CEO. The deal was finalized. *Today is Wednesday, a few more days, and I can go back to Rose and the kids*, Max thought with anticipation. Seeing that he has a little bit more time and wanting to celebrate buying a new company. He decided to get a cup of coffee before going back to work. He entered Caribou that was nearby.

Thankfully there was no line, so Max came to the front. "What can I get for you today?" said a woman with an annoyed tone.

While looking at the menu Max said, "May I have… " "Max is that you?" Asked the woman, shock evident in her voice. Max froze. That voice sounded somewhat familiar. Max looked at the woman shocked and alarm bells rang in his head. His only thought being, *No way!*

BONUS CHAPTER IS THIS LOVE?

DISCLAIMER! ROSE'S POINT OF VIEW

(10 years ago)

My mom and I helped Berda set up the table. *Dad is coming home finally!* I was not the only one surprised that dad wanted to make the trip personally, usually he would send Kyle, his vice-CEO I guess you could say, but not this time, I wonder why?

"Welcome to my mansion."

"Welcome home master Frank!" There stood three people. Max didn't know who they were but they seemed important. "Allow me to Introduce these three people, if it wasn't for them, then this mansion would cease to function". After that proceeded to Introduce his staff. Berda, the housekeeper. She was a woman with bright red hair, and was in her early 40's. It was clear that Berda served as Frank's housekeeper for a long time. Then there was Benjamin, the Butler. He was a man in his early 40's. He has black hair with streaks of gray hair. Finally, there was the chief, Luis. Luis is a fat man who loves to eat.

Maybe because of his love of food, he became a chief.

"If you need anything, please tell them"

"Dad, the food is getting cold!" I yelled from the kitchen. Dad walked into the kitchen with a man and a woman in to.

"Max, allow me toIntroduce you to my daughter, Rose". Dad gestured towards me with his hand. I found out that the man's name is Max. I extended my hand to Max out of politeness. It took him a while to shake it. I was confused. "Oh sorry" he murmured, shook my hand quickly and let go.

During dinner, Max kept staring at me, but the moment I look at him, he pretended like he wasn't staring at me. If that wasn't bad enough by the end of dinner, he stopped looking at me altogether. *Make up your damn mind already! Say something! Don't just stare!*

After the "staring incident" Max and I haven't spoken much. I feel like each of us is waiting for the other person to make the first move. One month has passed since Max came to live with us with his mom, Anna. During that time Max was successfully promoted from an intern to a regular employee. I thought that the promotion would be a cause for celebration, but I was wrong. Everyday Max would come home late and go to sleep right away. I was worried about him, so I talked to my dad when he got home one evening, "Dad can I talk to you?"

"Of course sweetie, what can I do for you?"

I hesitated a little before replying. My dad noticed my hesitation and said, Did something happen?"

"Dad, I am worried about Max. Is he alright? He comes home late. He barely has any time to rest. I am worried that he will over exert himself."

Frank listened to his daughter patiently and said, "Max has discipline and good work ethic. I am sure he will be fine. However, for your sake I will talk to the manager of his department."

Dad talked to Max's manager and his workload was lessened. I was glad. I saw it in his face too, the light has returned to his eyes. He wasn't as tired anymore. However, just when I thought that the worst was behind us, an incident occurred that changed my life: Max came home with blood stains on his shirt while his suit was in tatters. When I saw that I was near tears. "Max are you alright! What happened to you?"

"Rose, don't worry about me. Some dudes ambushed me on my way home. One of them had a knife. I was able to overpower all three, starting with the knife guy obviously. However, as a result, coming home unscathed became impossible."

"Don't scare me like that ever again you hear? I was worried sick. You're usually home by this point."

"You were worried about me? Why?" Asked Max confused and shocked at the same time.

"Because I…because I…I LOVE YOU, YOU IDIOT!" At this point I jumped into Max's arms and cried even harder. I wanted to confess for a while now, but usually the guy is supposed to make the first move, so I waited. However, today I realized that Max could have died. If that happened, then I would have regretted not confessing on time. However his next words shocked me the most, "I love you too"

After the "ambush incident" Dad launched a full investigation to find out who held a grudge against Max.

As it turns out, the person who hired the thugs was Kyle. Bob, the manager of Max's department was in cahoots with him. Also, Bob is the one that gave Max all that extra work, even though it wasn't his to begin with. It is only after Bob found out about Max's close relationship with Frank, that he stopped with the extra workload.

Kyle, as it turns out, had a crush on me, so when heard that the man I was supposedly living with worked in the same company, he instructed Bob to give Max more work. When that plan failed, Kyle hired some thugs to give Max a "warning". Furthermore, the investigation revealed that Kyle was in cahoots with our competitors and planning a hostile take over from the inside. Thankfully, that never came to pass. Both Kyle and Bob were fired immediately, while Ben and Max were promoted to manager and Vice-CEO respectively. Max proposed to me and I said yes. It was clear at this point that I was head-over-heels in love with Max, and I am 100% sure that he feels the same way. Now all we have to do is tell dad. Max and I walked into his office one evening while holding hands. "Daddy Max and I want to receive your blessings to be married" I said with determination. Dad saw the look in my eyes, then he turned towards Max and asked seriously, "Do you love my daughter?"

"Yes I do sir, very much" Max replied returning my dad's serious look. Satisfied with Max's reply dad stood up from his chair and said, "Be blessed my children. Seeingthe passion burning in both your eyes I will not delay marriage. The marriage will take place Sunday next week. Go, I will take care of everything. Oh and one more thing, don't delay having children. My wife and I want to see our grandchildren before me." When I heard "grandchildren" I blushed deeply. Dad saw me blushing and chuckled. After that his face turned serious once more. "I plan to retire in 10 years' time. I have decided to name Max as my successor. I will make the official announcement at the wedding." With that, both Max and I left the room in anticipation of our wedding day.

BONUS CHAPTER "I LOVE YOU"
DISCLAIMER! MAX'S POINT OF VIEW

"Welcome to my mansion!" I couldn't believe what I was seeing. The mansion was HUGE! Chandeliers on the ceiling. Leather couches everywhere. I was introduced to: Berta the housekeeper, Benjamin the Butler and Luis the head chef. Uncle Frank told me that if I needed anything to ask them. Next, my mom and I were introduced to Rose, uncle Frank's daughter. When I saw her I was stunned.

She had an elegant figure and waist length red hair. "Hey Max, are you alright?" My mom asked me and waved her hand in front of my face. "Hello! Earth to Max are you there?"

"Huh? Oh hi my name is Max". Rose extended her hand to shake mine. I took her hand in mine and didn't want to let go. Her hand was soft and smooth. Rose gave me a confused look, I noticed that I held her hand for too long. I immediately let go.

During dinner I couldn't stop staring at Rose. However, if she looks at me, I pretend to not look at her. *Stop it, you idiot! Have you learned nothing from Lily? Don't just pay attention to her looks!* Resist the urge to look at her.

Control yourself for crying out loud!

After dinner, Rose and I barely spoke to one-another. Choosing instead, to observe each other. Before I knew it, a month has passed since my mom and I moved in. At work, I was promoted to a regular employee from an intern. Also, I met Ben, a worker like myself. We became best friends instantly. We made a deal to help each other whenever possible. Therefore, whenever I would get overloaded with work, Ben would **help** me out. If it wasn't for him, I would have probably died from overexertion. Over the course of a month I worked like crazy. I came home very tired with barely any energy left. I noticed that Rose looks at me with worry in her eyes. "Are you alright? You seem exhausted."

"I am fine" I said, trying to play it off even though I was really tired. From that day forward, my life at work has gotten significantly easier. I found out that Frank stepped in and made sure that I would be getting work that was required, and nothing more. The only thing I thought of when I heard the news is *Thank you Rose*. Finally I could breath a sigh of relief.

Ever since I got here I made it a habit to run around at least once a week. I continued this pattern until I got ambushed. Apparently Bob my manager and Kyle[the vice-CEO] became wary of me after Frank stepped in to help me and decided that I was a threat that needed to be neutralized. I truly underestimated them. I went for a run just like any other. I guess these guys new my route and time. One of them even had a knife with him. Thankfully they were regular thugs. I focused on the one with the knife first. The others took advantage of the situation and when I attacked, the knife guy they attacked from either side. As a result I got minor cuts on my body, no bleeding. I was able to overpower all three in the end, but the blood of one of the thugs got on my suit. *Disgusting*. By the time I got home I was exhausted. That was my first real fight after all. *One wrong move, and I would have been dead.* That thought sent shivers down my spine. When I got home I heard, "Where were you? I was worried sick, you know!" I couldn't believe what I was hearing.

"Why were you worried about me?" I was surprised by my own question. *Why* do you even care why she was worried about you? *Did you forget* what Lily did to you? *It's not like Rose* loves you *right? No way!*

"Because I…because I…because I LOVE YOU! Don't scare me like that ever again!" Before I knew it, Rose jumped into my arms crying her eyes out. I comforted her the best I could by patting her head, and before I could stop them, the words naturally escaped my mouth, "I love you too." Rose lifted her head. Her face revealed a shocked expression, which was quickly replaced by a bright smile. I took my hand and gently removed the last tear Roses' face.

After the "ambush incident", Frank launched a full investigation. The investigation revealed that Kyle hired the three thugs for the ambush at Bob's request. It was also revealed that Kyle was planning a hostile takeover of the company with the help of our competitors. In the end, Both Bob and Kyle were fired from their jobs and sent to jail. Meanwhile, I replaced Kyle as the vice-CEO and Ben replaced Bob as the manager.

I LOVED YOU, YOU NEVER LOVED ME

(One month later)

I proposed to Rose. She said, "yes". After that we decided to get Frank's blessing on our union. We walked into Frank's office holding hands. Frank noticed this and waited for an explanation. "Daddy, Max and I decided to get married. Please bless our union." Frank looked at his daughter and saw determination in her eyes. Then he said to me, "Do you love my daughter?"

"Yes sir, with all of my heart." I replied with conviction.

Seeing how serious I was towards Rose, and knowing that Rose was head-over-heels in love with me he said, "I bless you, my children. Please don't delay with children. That is my last request. " When Rose heard that, she blushed crimson red, understanding exactly what her father implied.

"I will take care of everything. You two will be married in a week. Also, I plan to retire in 10 years, and I will name Max as my successor. I will make it official at the wedding." With that, Rose and I left the office holding hands waiting in anticipation for the big day. Frank had a big grin on his face

BONUS CHAPTER HAPPILY EVER AFTER.

"...With the power vested in me, I now pronounce you husband and wife. You may now kiss the bride. " Max kissed Rose and everyone cheered. *Finally! I achieved everything I wanted to achieve.* With these thoughts Max look at Rose, his wife and grinned to himself. What followed afterwards was a photoshoot of the bride and the groom. Next came the feast. Everyone was eating their fill. During this time, time was given for people to give their words of wisdom. After that, songs were sung and verses were told all giving the best of wishes to the young married couple. Then time was set aside for gift-giving. Most guests gave money as a gift. Finally at the end, came the ballroom dancing segment. The guests split into pairs and danced to slow, romantic music. Naturally, Max and Rose are in the middle. As they twirled around Max leaned in and whispered, "I love you" Rose blushed slightly and said, "I love you too. I hope you will take care of me." "I will do my best. I hope that you will give me children, so that our house is filled with laughter."

"I will do my best. From this day forth, I belong to you. I hope you will have me."

"That's my line." Standing there, surrounded by their guests, Max and Rose shared a passionate kiss.

AFTERWORD

Thank you for reading my latest book, I know that the book title, *I Loved You, You never Loved Me* is a cringe title, but please bare with me. Were you expecting the cliff hanger? However, here are the real questions: what happened to Lilly while Max was away for all these years? Does she regret leaving Max for another man? What happened to Jack after Max's accident? These questions and many more will be answered in the sequel, *I Loved You, but I made a Choice to leave*.

I am planning to write a book called, *I Borrowed you* as well as write a book, which will most likely turn into a project, called, *The Perfect Human*. The book is about chess. I hope to write this book with Gothemchess. Special Thanks to Dorrance Publishing for publishing this book. You guys are the best I will see you guys in my next book.

www.ingramcontent.com/pod-product-compliance
Lightning Source LLC
LaVergne TN
LVHW012103070526
838200LV00073BA/3409